Winner Takes ALL!

By Jodi Carse and Maria Gallagher

Illustrated by Brie Spangler

Poot!

Grosset & Dunlap ● New York

The REAL World

Sam hated mornings. Mornings meant two things: school and breakfast . . . and it was tough to decide which was worse. Now,  school was pretty awful—teachers, homework, and, ugh, girls. But breakfast . . . Sam and MJ's mom was a pretty lousy cook.  Her bacon was always burned black, her mashed potatoes were always lumpy, and her soup always tasted like smelly feet, no matter what was in it. So Sam always tried to move slowly in the mornings, hoping to put school and breakfast off for as long as possible.

First, he had to pack all the things
that he needed for school—

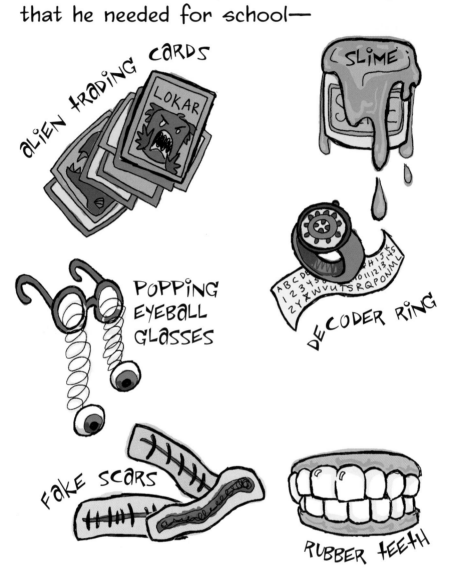

ALIEN TRADING CARDS

LOKAR

SLIME

DECODER RING

POPPING
EYEBALL
GLASSES

FAKE SCARS

RUBBER TEETH

oh, yeah, and his books
and pencil case.

Sam,
breakfast!

Then he had to get ready, which always took a *really* long time.

Bark! Bark!

Sam, what are you doing? Hurry up, or you won't have time to eat your breakfast!

Sam never knew what to expect at mealtime. Worst of all, his mom was trying something new—brain food. Sam sure hoped it wasn't made out of actual brains—but with his mom, anything was possible. No wonder he didn't want to come down to breakfast.

You almost missed your buckwheat soy spirulina pancake.

—SMAK!

THUD!

Why do we have to go through this every morning, Sam?

After Mom served up breakfast, Sam tried to distract her while he fed whatever she had cooked to the dog. Luckily, the dog would eat *anything*.

What time is it when the clock strikes thirteen? Time to get the clock fixed!
Here's the best one. I've been saving it for you . . . Mary was riding her bike when she knocked over a teacher. "Don't you know how to ride that thing yet?" he yelled. "Sure," she said. "It's the bell I don't know how to use!"
All done!
Um, okay, all ready, time to go, let's hit the road!
Wow, cool!
HYUCCCK

The Challenge

Monster, the, um, well, let's just say he's not the smartest

Gus, the unluckiest

Zip, the fastest

MJ, otherwise known as Sam's "evil twin"

Missy, the brain

Alex, the friendliest

Sam, the leader

Pru, the girly girl

At recess, Sam told the Stinky Boys Club about his dream. The Stinky Boys were Sam's best friends and partners in crime. They started a club to get away from girls . . . especially MJ and her friends.

"It really was the best dream ever. I mean, imagine if *everything* you ever wished for suddenly came true," Sam said.

"Likewinningthesoccerchampionship!" Zip said.

The Plan

After school, the boys went back to their super-duper-top-secret-no-girls-allowed-at-all clubhouse to come up with a plan to beat the girls *once and for all.* Sam turned to Joe Computer, the master computer he had built. Joe suggested that a competition would be the best way to prove that boys were better than girls.

Zip ran off to give the girls the rules. Each side had to come up with three events— tests of intelligence, strength . . .

and grossness!

Joe bleeped and BLIPPED and blooped and flashed and flickered and bleeped and blipped some more and FLASHED again and . . .

BOYS VS. GIRLS COMPETITION

EVENT #1
AN EATING CONTEST

EVENT #2
A BURPING CONTEST

EVENT #3
A JOKE CONTEST

GIRLS vs. BOYS

A quiz

A knitting contest

A dare

May the best **GIRL** win!

Let the Games Begin

The eating contest was first. The winner had to eat the most fried baloney sandwiches in five minutes to win.

FRIED BALONEY SANDWICH

Have you ever had a fried baloney sandwich? It's a truly gross treat! Ask an adult to help you make one.

For each sandwich, you will need:
- 2 slices baloney
- 2 pieces white bread
- 1 tsp. oil

1. Have an adult cut four slits in the baloney from the edge toward the center (like slicing a pie—but don't cut all the way to the center).

2. Place baloney in a frying pan that has been thinly coated with oil. Ask an adult to fry the baloney for about 5 minutes over medium heat.

Delicious!

3. Put the baloney between the two slices of bread. Mayonnaise or peanut butter will make it extra-gross and greasy!

Not that Zip needed five minutes. He had already eaten twenty fried baloney sandwiches in less than two minutes.

Now you might think it is easy to burp, since it's something everyone can do. You have probably seen your dad burp, and maybe even your teacher. But to do it right takes concentration and skill. Monster was famous for his burps. He could burp anyone's name, or burp a song. He could do a sneeze-burp and hiccup-burp and the ever-popular burp-fart combination. And when he really tried, he could burp the deepest, loudest, jump-out-of-your-skin burps that sounded like they were coming from a monster, which, by the way, is how he got his nickname.

Ha-Choo! BURP!

Nice one, Monster! We'll win for sure.

BUUUUUURP!

Re-Group

Since the kids were going on a field trip to the Lost Caverns in a few days, their quiz would be on caves. Now caves are cool, but everybody knows that the coolest things about caves are bats.

And bats are something girls don't like. So I programmed Joe to only ask questions about bats.

The boys stayed up late reading lots of questions about bats.
1. Bats are blind—true or false?
2. How do bats find their way and locate prey?
3. Are most bats cruel by nature?
4. Do vampire bats really drink blood?

1. Bats are not blind; many can see very well. So don't call someone "blind as a bat," because it's not true! 2. Bats depend on sound and have very good hearing which helps them get around in the dark. 3. No, bats are generally shy and afraid of humans. Just think how big you look to a bat! 4. Vampire bats do drink the blood of small animals to survive. But don't worry, they don't drink human blood!

1. What is the difference between a stalactite and a stalagmite?

2. What is a spelunker?

3. _____ is a type of rock found in many caves.

Oh, no! There are barely any questions about bats! What went wrong?

Time's up!

1. Stalactites are the cone-shaped structures that form at the top of the cave and hang downward. Stalagmites are like stalactites, but they form on the floor of the cave and grow upward. 2. A person who explores caves. 3. Limestone.

Joe graded all the tests, and just as everyone expected, Missy won.

Knit-Wit

The next competition was the knitting contest. Pru invited the Stinky Boys over to her house.

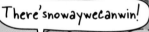

Pru's bedroom is a lot like Pru. Everything is pink and girly and smells like strawberries. It's filled with all the things she loves—teddy bears, ponies, and posters of cute boy bands (and Sam!). Basically, it is the last place on Earth the boys would **ever** want to be.

Zip and Monster somehow got their yarn tangled together.

But Sam was off to a good start—a very good start.

And Gus was a disaster.

His scarf was getting longer and longer.

In fact, Sam was in the lead, until . . .

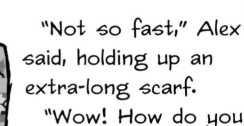

"Not so fast," Alex said, holding up an extra-long scarf.

"Wow! How do you know how to knit?" Sam exclaimed.

"Oh, I've taken a few classes," replied Alex.

"I'll definitely win the joke contest tomorrow," Sam said. "Soon everyone will know that boys really are the best!"

Now they were tied:

Score

Boys 2
Girls 2

The Joke's on You

Sam and MJ decided to have the joke contest during their class field trip to the Lost Caverns. Sam brought his laff-o-meter to measure the laughs. He just knew he would win—after all, Sam has been collecting jokes since first grade. He has over 2,674 of the world's best jokes!

MJ had had to listen to Sam's jokes all day, every day, sometimes five times a day. Just because she didn't laugh at them didn't mean she wasn't paying attention.

Sam knew he was in trouble. He knew he had only one more shot to win the contest. But that made Sam so nervous that he couldn't remember his own jokes.

Dare You

Sam had never been in a cave before, but he had learned a lot about them in class. Caves are cool, almost as cool as bats. The walls are slimy and all kinds of gross and freaky creatures live there in the dark.

Cave spiders, beetles, amphipods, and of course bats . . .

Going Batty

The boys walked deeper into the tunnel until there was no more light. It's funny how much louder things sound in the dark. They could hear the sound of water dripping, small insects scurrying across the floor, wind blowing through a hole, the rustling of the bat wings, and the pounding of their hearts.

But it's across a stream and very high up. . .

Well, it sounds like our best chance. Let's give it a try.

 The kids walked and walked until they reached the stream, which was full of fish and amphipods.

It's not that deep. We could probably walk across.

No way.

Plus, we don't want to disturb this natural habitat.

Alex, give me your scarf.

Sam tried to throw one end of the scarf onto a stalactite across the stream, but his aim was always a little off. Luckily, MJ was the champion pitcher on the baseball team. Unluckily, she never let him forget it.

Don't worry, everyone. I'll do it.

One by one, the kids swung across the stream and landed on the other side.

Back in the Light

How will we get Monster out?

Sam dropped one end of the scarf down to Monster. He wrapped the other end around a tree.

Well, everyone knows boys are better than girls.
No way! Everyone knows girls are better than boys.
Are not.
Are too.
Are NOT.
Are TOO.
ARE NOT!
the End
for Now